For my friends
Bobbie, Sandra and Sarah Jane,
with love and gratitude

With thanks also to Paul and Sylvie
for all their kind help

First published 2002 by Walker Books Ltd
87 Vauxhall Walk, London SE11 5HJ

2 4 6 8 10 9 7 5 3 1

© 2002 Simon James

The right of Simon James to be identified as author
of this work has been asserted by him in accordance
with the Copyright, Designs and Patents Act 1988

This book has been typeset in Garamond ITC Book Condensed

Printed in Italy

British Library Cataloguing in Publication Data:
a catalogue record for this book is available
from the British Library

ISBN 0-7445-7592-3

# The Birdwatchers

## Simon James

WALKER BOOKS

AND SUBSIDIARIES

LONDON • BOSTON • SYDNEY

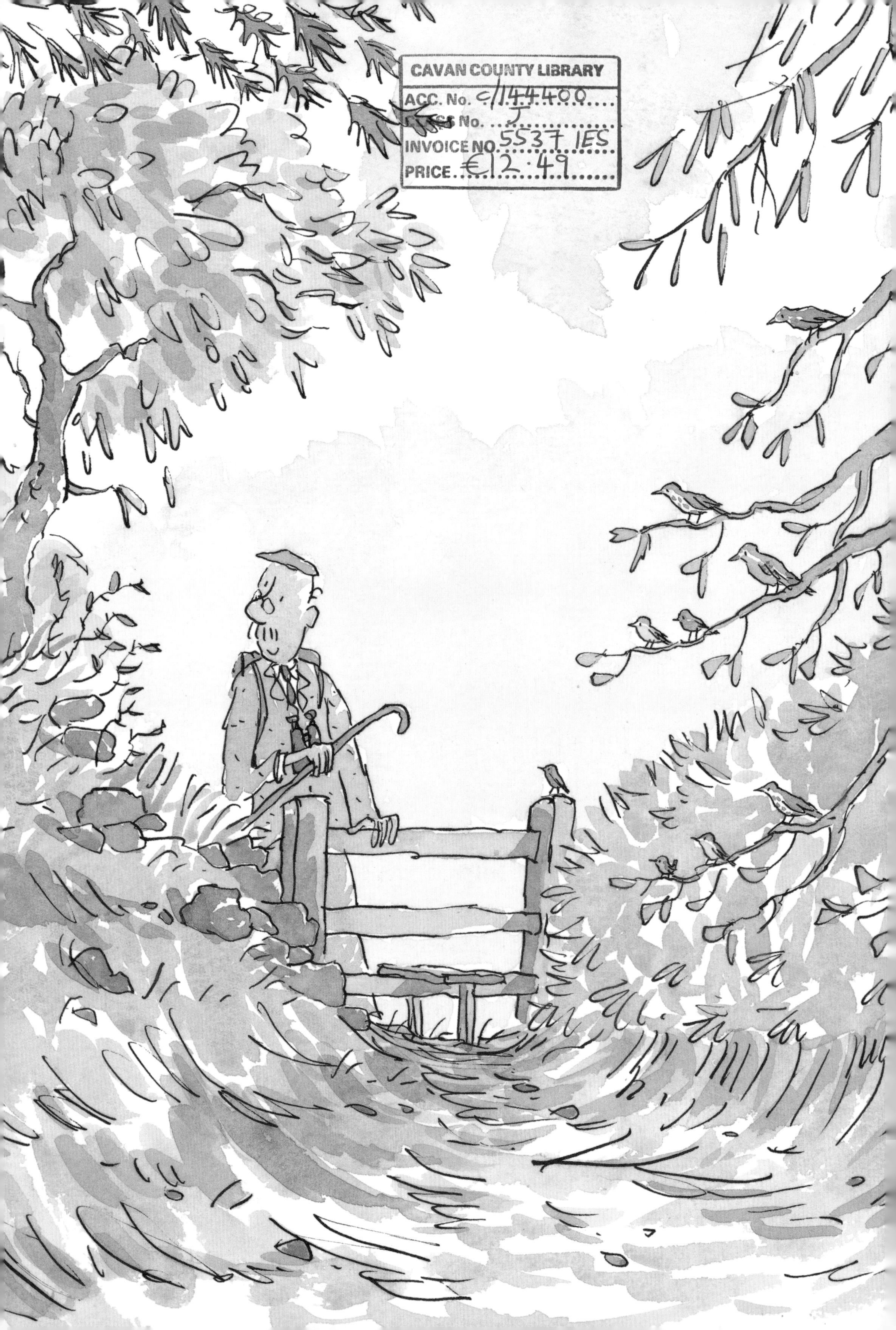

My grandad is a birdwatcher.

He tells me birdwatching stories.

He always says, "Jess, when I go

birdwatching, things happen."

Once my grandad said,
"Jess, when I make drawings
of the birds, sometimes they
make drawings of me, too."

My grandad said, "Jess,
sometimes the birds help me
when I can't find their names
in my bird book."

And my grandad said, "Jess,
I got all the birds together
one morning to record
something called the
dawn chorus, just for you."

My grandad said,
"Birds are amazing, Jess."
But I wasn't sure. I had
to find out for myself.

So one day I decided to go
birdwatching with him.
When we got there, I couldn't
believe it.

I couldn't see anything at all.

Grandad showed me how to use
his binoculars. Everything was
closer. But I couldn't see anything.
Nothing happened.

Then Grandad took me
to the bird-hide.

Grandad opened the hatch
and we looked out.
It was amazing.

I'd never seen so many birds.
Grandad said there were tufted
ducks, herons, sedge warblers,
snipe and crested grebes.
We made lots of notes and
loads of drawings.

Soon it was time to go.
On the way back Grandad
asked me what I liked best
about my first day birdwatching.

That's when I thought
I'd tell him a birdwatching
story of my own.

"Grandad, I liked it best when
the dancing penguins came
and shared my sandwich."

"Dancing penguins, Jess?"
said Grandad.
"I must have been
looking the other way."

The End